# The Little Engine That Could™
# STORYBOOK TREASURY

Platt & Munk, Publishers

Copyright © 1930, 1945, 1954, 1961, 1976, 1988, 1993, 2000, 2001, 2002, 2003 by Platt & Munk, Publishers.
All rights reserved. Published by Platt & Munk, Publishers, an imprint of Grosset & Dunlap, which is
a division of Penguin Young Readers Group, 345 Hudson Street, New York, NY 10014.
THE LITTLE ENGINE THAT COULD, engine design, "I THINK I CAN," and PLATT & MUNK are trademarks
of Penguin Group (USA) Inc. Registered in U.S. Patent and Trademark Office.
Published simultaneously in Canada. Manufactured in China.

*Library of Congress Cataloging-in-Publication Data*
Piper, Watty, pseud.
The little engine that could storybook treasury / based on the original story by Watty Piper.
p. cm.
Summary: A collection of seven tales featuring the Little Blue Engine, who is best known for
trying to pull a load of stranded toys over the mountain despite her being so small.
[1. Railroads—Trains—Fiction.] I. Title.
PZ7.P64   Lr   2003   [E]—dc21   2002014387

ISBN 0-448-43114-9       B C D E F G H I J

# The Little Engine That Could™
## STORYBOOK TREASURY

**Based on the original story by Watty Piper**

Includes **7** of the Most Popular
The Little Engine That Could™ Stories

*Platt & Munk, Publishers*

# TABLE OF CONTENTS

# THE LITTLE ENGINE THAT COULD™

Retold by
**Watty Piper**

*Illustrated by*
*George & Doris Hauman*

Chug, chug, chug. Puff, puff, puff. Ding-dong, ding-dong. The little train rumbled over the tracks.

She was a happy little train for she had such a jolly load to carry. Her cars were filled full of good things for boys and girls.

There were toy animals—giraffes with long necks, Teddy bears with almost no necks at all, and even a baby elephant.

Then there were dolls—dolls with blue eyes and yellow curls,
dolls with brown eyes and brown bobbed heads, and the funniest
little toy clown you ever saw.

And there were cars full of toy engines, airplanes, tops, jackknives, picture puzzles, books, and every kind of thing boys or girls could want.

But that was not all. Some of the cars were filled
with all sorts of good things for boys and girls to
eat—big golden oranges, red-cheeked apples,

bottles of creamy milk for their breakfasts, fresh
spinach for their dinners, peppermint drops, and
lollypops for after-meal treats.

The little train was carrying all these wonderful things to the good little boys and girls on the other side of the mountain.

She puffed along merrily. Then all of a sudden she stopped with a jerk. She simply could not go another inch. She tried and she tried, but her wheels would not turn.

What were all those good little boys and girls on the other side of the mountain going to do without the wonderful toys to play with and the good food to eat?

"Here comes a shiny new engine," said the funny little clown
who jumped out of the train.
"Let us ask him to help us."

So all the dolls and toys cried out together, "Please, Shiny New Engine, won't you please pull our train over the mountain? Our engine has broken down, and the boys and girls on the

other side won't have any toys to play with or good food
to eat unless you help us."

But the Shiny New Engine snorted: "I pull you? I am a Passenger Engine. I have just carried a fine big train over the mountain, with more cars than you ever dreamed of. My train had sleeping cars, with comfortable berths; a dining car where

waiters bring whatever hungry people want to eat; and parlor cars in which people sit in soft armchairs and look out of big plate-glass windows. I pull the likes of you? Indeed not!"

And off he steamed to the roundhouse, where engines
live when they are not busy. How sad the little train and all
the dolls and toys felt!

Then the little clown called out, "The Passenger Engine is not the only one in the world. Here is another engine coming, a great big strong one. Let us ask him to help us."

The little toy clown waved his flag and the big strong
engine came to a stop.

"Please, oh, please, Big Engine," cried all the dolls and toys
together. "Won't you please pull our train over the mountain?

Our engine has broken down, and the good little boys and girls on the other side won't have any toys to play with or good food to eat unless you help us."

But the Big Strong Engine bellowed: "I am a Freight Engine.
I have just pulled a big train loaded with big machines over the
mountain. These machines print books and newspapers for

grown-ups to read. I am a very important engine indeed.
I won't pull the likes of you!" And the Freight Engine
puffed off indignantly to the roundhouse.

The little train and all the dolls and toys were very sad.
"Cheer up," cried the little toy clown. "The Freight Engine is
not the only one in the world. Here comes another. He looks very

old and tired, but our train is so little, perhaps he can help us."

So the little toy clown waved his flag and the dingy, rusty old engine stopped.

"Please, Kind Engine," cried all the dolls and toys together. "Won't you please pull our train over the mountain? Our engine has broken down, and the boys and girls on the other side won't have any toys to play with or good food to eat unless you help us."

But the Rusty Old Engine sighed, "I am so tired. I must rest

my weary wheels. I cannot pull even so little a train as yours
over the mountain. I can not. I can not."

And off he rumbled to the roundhouse chugging, "I can not.
I can not. I can not."

Then indeed the little train was very, very sad, and the dolls and toys were ready to cry.

But the little clown called out, "Here is another engine coming, a little blue engine, a very little one, maybe she will help us."

The very little engine came chug, chugging merrily along. When she saw the toy clown's flag, she stopped quickly.

"What is the matter, my friends?" she asked kindly.

"Oh, Little Blue Engine," cried the dolls and toys. "Will you pull us over the mountain? Our engine has broken down and the good boys and girls on the other side won't have any toys to play with

or good food to eat, unless you help us. Please, please help us, Little Blue Engine."

"I'm not very big," said the Little Blue Engine. "They use me only for switching trains in the yard. I have never been over the mountain."

"But we must get over the mountain before the children awake," said all the dolls and the toys.

The very little engine looked up and saw the tears in the dolls' eyes. And she thought of the good little boys and girls on the other side of the mountain who would not have any toys or good food unless she helped.

Then she said, "I think I can. I think I can. I think I can."
And she hitched herself to the little train.

She tugged and pulled and pulled and tugged and slowly, slowly, slowly they started off.

The toy clown jumped aboard and all the dolls and the toy animals began to smile and cheer.

Puff, puff, chug, chug, went the Little Blue Engine. "I think I can—I think I can—I think I can—I think I can—I think I can—I think I can—I think I can—I think I can—I think I can."

Up, up, up. Faster and faster and faster the little engine climbed, until at last they reached the top of the mountain.

Down in the valley lay the city.

"Hurray, hurray," cried the funny little clown and all the dolls and toys. "The good little boys and girls in the city will be happy because you helped us, kind Little Blue Engine."

And the Little Blue Engine smiled **and seemed** to say as she puffed steadily down the mountain . . .

"I thought I could. I thought I could. I thought I could.
I thought I could.
                    I thought I could.
                                        I thought I could."

# The Little Engine That Could™
## AND THE BIG CHASE

By Michaela Muntean

Illustrated by Florence Graham

The Little Blue Engine worked in the train yard on the other side of the mountain. She was very happy there because she had many friends who came to visit her.

Whenever the dolls came, they would polish her brass bell until it shone like gold.

And whenever the monkey, the baby elephant, the teddy bears, and the giraffes came, they would give the Little Blue Engine a bath so that she would always look her best.

First, the baby elephant would spray the Little Blue Engine with water from his trunk.

Then the teddy bears would rub the Little Blue Engine dry—and the giraffes would dry all the parts that the teddy bears couldn't reach!

The monkey would scrub all the ticklish spots, like inside the Little Blue Engine's smokestack.

Soon that little engine would be as bright blue as a the sky on a sunny summer day!

The Little Blue Engine loved her friends and her friends loved her.

But her very best friend was the little toy clown.

"It would not matter if it was snowing or raining or sleeting," the toy clown would always say. "It would not matter if there was a hurricane or a flood up to my eyeballs. I would be here every day."

And so he was.

Every day, the clown would walk across the train yard until he reached the Little Blue Engine. Then he would climb up and settle down behind her smokestack.

Sometimes the clown would tell the Little Blue Engine a joke that would make her laugh, *chiggity-chiggle, chiggity-chig.* Sometimes he would read her a story.

But on most days, they would just talk.

They would talk about faraway train tracks that led to faraway places, and about the adventures they would have getting there.

The little clown and the Little Blue Engine had big dreams.

One day, the clown decided to do something new to make the Little Blue Engine laugh. Instead of walking through the train yard as he usually did, he hopped from the top of one engine to the next, slowly making his way toward his friend.

"Look at me!" he called as he did a handstand on top of a shiny silver engine. Then he somersaulted onto a small yellow engine. From there, he did a backflip onto a big strong engine.

The Little Blue Engine laughed and laughed.

But as the toy clown stood on the Big Strong Engine waving at his friend, the Big Strong Engine suddenly pulled out of the train yard! "Stop!" cried the clown. But the Big Strong Engine, with all its *huffing* and *puffing* and *chugging* and *chooing*, did not hear him.

"Hang on!" the Little Blue Engine called to her friend. "I'll get help!"

The Big Strong Engine was so strong and so fast, he was soon out of the train yard with his cargo behind him—and a little toy clown riding on top of him.

The Little Blue Engine had to do something—
and she had to do it fast!

*Toot-toot!* She sounded her whistle.

*Clangity-clang!* She rang her bell.

In the city, all of her friends heard the familiar sound of the bell.

"That's the Little Blue Engine," the dolls said.

"And it sounds like something is wrong," the teddy bears said to the giraffes.

"We had better see what's the matter," the baby elephant said to the monkey.

So they all hurried to the train yard.

When they arrived, the Little Blue Engine told them what had happened.

"We have to catch that big engine," she said.

The Small Yellow Engine overheard her. "*Choo-choo-hoo-ha!*" he snorted. "That big engine is the strongest and fastest engine in the yard. He is traveling far into the country to deliver seeds and tools to the farmers. The likes of you could never catch the likes of him!"

But the Little Blue Engine was going to try, and off she went, *chuggity-chug*, with all her friends on board.

They started off slowly, and then the Little Blue Engine tried to go faster. "I think I can. I think I can. I think I can," she said as she sped along the tracks.

Up ahead was a long, dark tunnel. The giraffes bent their heads low.

The dolls and the baby elephant shut their eyes tight. But the Little Blue Engine did not have time to be afraid. She had to catch that engine and save her friend.

"I think I can. I think I can. I think I can," she said as she raced through that long, dark tunnel.

On the other side of the tunnel were tracks leading in two different directions. Beside the tracks sat an old caboose.

"Oh, Caboose," said the Little Blue Engine, "can you tell me which way the Big Strong Engine went? I have to catch him."

"He went that way," said the Old Caboose. "But he was going very fast and there is bad weather ahead. You will never catch him."

But the Little Engine was going to try, and off she went again, huffing and puffing as fast as she could.

The Old Caboose was right about the weather. The wind began to blow and the rain began to fall hard and fast.

"Be careful," cried the dolls, "or your wheels will jump off the tracks."

But the Little Blue Engine could think only about the toy clown.

*It would not matter if there was a hurricane or flood up to my eyeballs,* the clown had said. *I would be here every day.*

So on rode the brave Little Blue Engine. "I think I can. I think I can. I think I can," she said as the rain splashed all around her.

The giraffes with their long necks were keeping watch. Soon they let out a cheer.

"The Big Strong Engine is just ahead of us!" they cried.

The Little Blue Engine went faster and faster until . . . she was riding right next to the Big Strong Engine! And there, on the top, she could see a very wet and tired clown.

All the other toys were ready with their rescue plan. The elephant gave everyone a boost. The monkey hung on to a teddy bear, who hung on to a doll, who hung onto a giraffe's neck.

"Grab my tail," the monkey called to the clown, and together they pulled the toy clown onto the Little Blue Engine.

"Hooray! We did it!" they all cheered as the tired Little Blue Engine came to a stop.

"You got here just in time," said the clown. "I don't think I could have held on much longer."

They waited until the skies were clear. Then very slowly they headed back to the city on the other side of the mountain.

As she huffed and puffed steadily along the track, the Little Blue Engine smiled and seemed to say . . .

"I thought I could. I thought I could. I thought I could."

And the toy clown answered . . .

"I knew you would. I knew you would. I knew you would."

# The Little Engine That Could™
# ABC
## TIME

illustrated by
Cristina Ong

I'm the Little Blue Engine, singing the ABCs!
Will you take an alphabet train trip with me?
Just follow my train tracks
and guess what you'll see?
All the alphabet letters
from A right through Z!

# A

Let's start in the meadow
where boys and girls play.
Can you find a fruit
that begins with an A?

For B, look and find a most beautiful thing—
It flies past the flowers on colorful wings.

Answers are on page 104 and 105!

Over the hill we go!
Come, follow me.
At the circus, find someone
whose name starts with C.
For D, find a little pet fetching a stick.
Will he get a treat for his clever trick?

D

E

Under the big top are the next letters we seek.
As we roll by, let's all take a peek!
E is a big animal with a long, gray snout.
F is for a kind of banner waving about.

On the farm, the letters G and H will appear.
Find the animal that made the footprints here.
Then look for a creature that's gentle and strong,
With a pretty brown mane and a tail so long.

Follow me to the park and find I, J, and K.
Now what's fun to eat on a hot summer day?
Can you see a jumping game that kids like to play,
and a toy with a tail that flies up and away?

J

K

Next on our trip, we'll stop at the zoo.
For L, there's a cat that's much bigger than you.
M is an animal swinging up high.
Can you find them both as we go chugging by?

For N and O, come to the schoolyard with me.
What do the children see inside the tree?
High in the branches, there's an animal, too—
It stays up all night and says *whoo-whoo-whoo!*

P

At the country fair there are good things to eat—
Like a nice dessert treat that starts with a P.
There are pony rides, balloons, and crafts for sale, too.
Do you see a blanket that starts with a Q?

Here at the picnic are the letters R and S.
Now let's see if you will pass this little test:
Find a long-eared critter that likes carrots to munch,
And a food that the children will have for their lunch.

Follow me to the beach and we'll find T and U.
For T, I see fun things to play with—do you?
For U, look around for a nice, shady spot;
Kids can sit beneath it when the sun is too hot.

Now we'll head to the post office—that's what we'll do.
There we'll find V, and W, too.
Do you see a sweet card from somebody's friend?
And something to carry a big package in?

# X

Come along to the toy store to find the last three—
The end of the alphabet: X, Y, and Z.
There's a musical instrument,
and a toy on a string.
And a black-and-white animal
is the very last thing.

You've found every letter. I'm so proud of you!
But before I go, here is what we should do:
Let's make a long alphabet train out of me—
I'll pull all the letters and sing A, B, C!

A is for apple.
B is for butterfly.
C is for clown.
D is for dog.
E is for elephant.
F is for flag.

G is for goat.
H is for horse.
I is for ice cream.
J is for jump rope.
K is for kite.
L is for lion.

M is for monkey.
N is for nest.
O is for owl.
P is for pie.
Q is for quilt.
R is for rabbit.
S is for sandwich.

T is for toys.
U is for umbrella.
V is for valentine.
W is for wagon.
X is for xylophone.
Y is for yo-yo.
Z is for zebra.

Our train trip is over!
I'm glad as can be
That you could come
with me from A to Z.

# The Little Engine That Could™

# LET'S COUNT
# 1-2-3

illustrated by
Cristina Ong

Chug, chug, chug. Puff, puff, puff.
The Little Blue Engine is on her way
to pick up all her friends today.
They're going on a special trip.

1 monkey is coming along.

Can you find 1 flower
and 1 bird in this picture?

Who is waiting by
the cozy cottage?

2 pretty dolls!

Do you see 2 sunflowers,
and 2 round windows?

Toot! Toot! Toot! Is anybody in the windmill?

Yes, there are 3 Dutch boys.

Look for 3 cats and 3 shovels
in this picture.

Puff, puff, puff.
All aboard!

4 teddy bears are ready
to hop onto the train.

Can you find 4 elephants and 4 zebras?

Who is coming aboard next?

5 tall giraffes want
to come for the ride.

Where are 5 tigers?

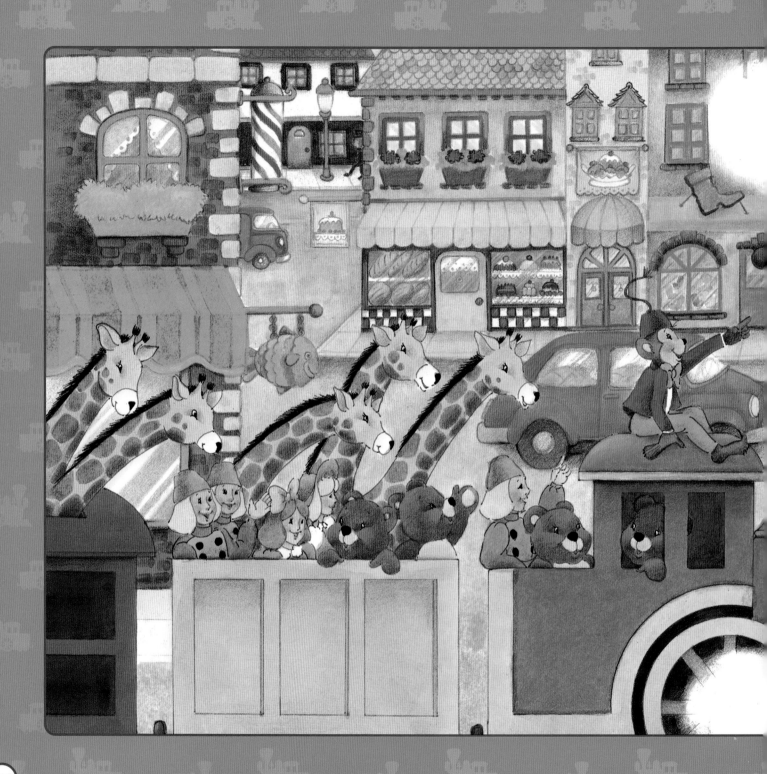

6 toy soldiers march on board.

Look for 6 cakes and 6 flowers in this picture.

**6**

In the busy town the Little Blue Engine stops at the toy store.

Mr. Egg is ready at the train station.

He brings 7 funny hats.

Can you see 7 suitcases and 7 crates?

Chug, chug, chug. The Little Blue Engine rumbles through the countryside.

**8**

"Cheep, cheep, cheep!
We'll come too,"
chirp 8 bluebirds.

8 bunnies are hiding
somewhere in this picture!

"I'm almost there. I'm almost there," chugs the Little Blue Engine.

"Quack! Quack!
Where are you going?"
ask 9 ducklings.

Look for 9 cows.
Look for 9 turtles.

They're going to the circus!
Everyone wants to see the star of the show.

It's the toy clown
juggling 10 balls.

Can you find 10 flags?

Let the circus parade begin!
Can you count all the
Little Blue Engine's friends?

# The Little Engine That Could™
# SOUNDS ALL AROUND

illustrated by Cristina Ong

# Chug! Chug!

What's that sound?

The Little Blue Engine is coming to town!

Boom! Boom!
The drummer hits the drums.

Clang! Clang!
Time to bang the cymbals!

Beep! Beep!
All the cars stop to say hello!

Honk! Honk!
Look! Now there is a traffic jam!

Quack! Quack!
The ducks swim back and forth.

Woof! Woof!
A dog barks happily.

Waah! Waah!
The baby cries in the crowd.

Shhh! Shhh!
The Little Blue Engine has to leave soon.

Toot! Toot!
The Little Blue Engine says good-bye!

# The Little Engine That Could™
## BABY ANIMALS

illustrated by Cristina Ong

The Little Blue Engine is ready to go!
Hop on board...

Where are they going?

To pick up baby animals at the zoo!

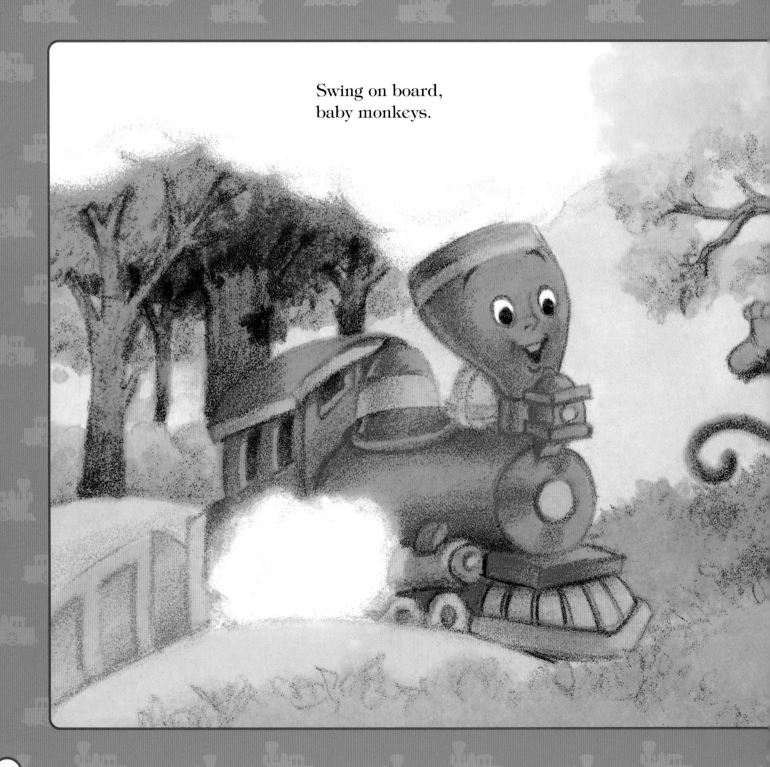

Swing on board,
baby monkeys.

Hello, baby elephants!
Come ride with us!

Baby giraffes have long necks!

They want to come, too!

Baby zebras gallop to meet the other animals.

Hop on board!

Where is the Little Blue Engine taking them?

To the circus!

# The Little Engine That Could™
## AND THE LOST HIPPO

illustrated by
Cristina Ong

Hal is sad. Hal is lost.

Where is Mommy?
Where is Daddy?

Here is a train yard.
Who lives here?

The Little Blue Engine!

Hal looks
and looks.

He wants to be with his mommy and daddy.

Can the Little
Blue Engine help?

Yes.
She will try.

They go over the river.

I think I can.
I think I can.

They go up a hill.
*Chug, chug, chug!*
I think I can. I think I can!

Oh, look!
There is Mommy!
There is Daddy!

Now they go down the hill.
*Puff, puff, puff.*

Hal is happy!

Hurray for the Little Blue Engine!